D0577042

The Prog Frince

A Mixed-Up Tale

BY C. Drew Lamm

ILLUSTRATED BY

Barbara McClintock

ORCHARD BOOKS
NEW YORK

Here's to Ellery Rose,
Steven Russell,
and
anyone who has lips,
pockets,
been a frog,
read a muffin,
eaten a story,
is not so green,
has leapt,
can say "poured a portion of potion"
three times fast . . .
or
is smiling now.
—C.D.L.

To Kathleen
—B.M.

Orchard Books, A Grolier Company, 95 Madison Avenue, New York, NY 10016

Manufactured in the United States of America
Printed and bound by Phoenix Color Corp. Book design by Mina Greenstein.
The text of this book is set in 16 point Cochin. The illustrations are pen and ink and watercolor.
1 3 5 7 9 10 8 6 4 2

Library of Congress Cataloging-in-Publication Data
Lamm, C. Drew. The Prog Frince / by C. Drew Lamm ;
illustrated by Barbara McClintock. p. cm.
Summary: When Jane sets off for the bakery to buy a muffin one morning, in her pocket she finds an enchanted frog wearing her dime for a hat.
ISBN 0-531-30135-4 (trade : alk. paper).—ISBN 0-531-33135-0 (lib. bdg. : alk. paper)
[1. Fairy tales. 2. Frogs—Fiction.] I. McClintock, Barbara, ill. II. Title.
PZ8.L1386Pr 1999 [E]—dc21 98-12379

Jane woke up thinking, Muffins! She dumped her pony bank onto her bed and silver coins rolled out. Jane placed them in the left front pocket of her frock and set off for the bakery.

As she turned the corner, her pocket moved. Jane walked faster. Her pocket jumped twice.

Jane reached the bakery and headed for the muffins. The left front pocket of her frock leapt up and down. Jane stopped. She put her hand carefully into her pocket and touched something. It was soft and slightly wet. She turned around, marched past the pies, and out the door. Jane shoved her hand back into her pocket and pulled out a frog. It was green, of course, and wore a dime on its head.

Jane frowned. "Is that my dime?" she said.

"It might have been," said the frog. "But it's my hat now."

"Give it back," Jane demanded. She poked the frog and tried to snatch the dime off his head.

"You're not a princess, are you?" said the frog.

"We don't have princesses in this village," explained Jane.

"How about talking frogs?" asked the frog.

"There aren't any of those anywhere," she said.

"Unfortunate," said the frog.

"Where's my—"

"Do you read fairy tales," interrupted the frog, "like *The Frog Prince*?"

"No," said Jane. "They don't make sense. And they're not true."

"What do you dream about?" he asked.

"I don't," said Jane.

"What do you do?"

"I go to school," she said, glaring at the frog.

"Unfortunate," croaked the frog, and he leapt off Jane's hand.

"Stop thief!" yelled Jane.

A window of a nearby house swung open, and an old woman with eyes as dark as horse chestnuts peered out.

"Having a problem?" she called.

"Help!" shouted Jane. "My muffin money turned into a frog and it's escaping with my dime on his head and—"

"Do you know the story *The Boy Who Cried Wolf*?" interrupted the woman.

"No," frowned Jane. "I don't like made-up stories."

"Well, you have two things to learn," muttered the old woman. "One: Don't call for help when you don't need any. Two: Read stories." And she swung the window shut.

By this time the frog had reached the edge of the stream. As Jane ran up, the frog leapt for a branch floating in the middle.

He missed.

"Come back here!" cried Jane.
She stood on the bank and scowled.

The frog emerged, coughed twice, and settled himself on the opposite bank.

"Don't do that frowning thing," he said.

"I want muffins and I can't buy muffins with a frog." Then Jane thought for a moment. Perhaps there was something about frogs that she had not learned in school.

"Is there some sort of rhyme I'm supposed to say, or something I should do? What about that *Prog Frince* you asked me about?"

"Frog Prince," said the frog. "It's a long story." He settled himself underneath a leaf. "Do you want to hear it?" he asked.

"Would it help?"

"Stories always help," replied the frog.

"All right," said Jane. "Tell me *The Prog Frince.*"

"Frog Prince!" said the frog.

Jane sat on the edge of the stream and rested her chin on her left knee.

"Once upon a time," began the frog, "in a land not so far away, lived a kind and gentle prince. The prince lived in a palace with his royal parents and millions of murals, mirrors, marionettes, mattresses, medallions, measuring sticks, moneybags, musicians, maroon marbles, and muffins."

Jane raised her hand. "Is this true?"

"Although the prince had the entire castle to play in," continued the frog, "he chose the stables. The prince loved carrying hay to the royal horses. That was really the job of a stable girl named Jaylee. But she didn't mind. She liked the prince. Each morning Jaylee and the prince fed the horses together. The job was done in twice the time."

"In winter they caught snow on their tongues. When the snow was thick, they threw snowballs at each other and sometimes at the castle windows, although they weren't supposed to."

"In spring they spent splashing days beside the stream. They floated twigs as boats and raced them in the rushing water. On warm, stormy days they danced in the rain."

"In summer they swam in the lake. They dove for pebbles and floated dandelions in patterns on the surface."

"And no matter the season or weather, they made up songs, read fairy tales, and played tag."

"Then one summer evening, just before bed, the king called the prince into his royal chamber.

'You are a man now, my son, and you must fall in love.'

'All right,' said the prince. 'I love Jaylee.'

'I'm serious,' said the king. 'We will hold a ball and invite the kindest and bravest princesses in the land to come dance with you. If she will have you, the princess who makes you smile shall be your bride.'

'I'm smiling now,' said the prince.

'We shall discuss this further in the morning,' replied his father.

But the prince always said the same thing whenever the king mentioned the ball.

'I'm smiling now,' he would answer.

So the king began to watch the prince and Jaylee. His son smiled so easily with the stable girl. His cheeks blushed roses, and his laughter echoed off the courtyard walls. But Jaylee was not a princess.

'Unfortunate,' muttered the king."

"Early one morning the king set off into the dark woods. He passed the fork in the stream just before midday and reined in his royal steed underneath a horse chestnut tree. As the sun reached the summit of the sky, the tree quivered. Half of the great trunk lowered into a drawbridge. Inside sat an old woman. She wore a string of horse chestnuts around her neck and had tied some onto her fingers as rings. The king entered the tree."

“‘Having a problem Your Majesty?’ she crackled.

‘It is time for my son to marry,’ replied the king. ‘But he has fallen in love with a common girl. I need an anti-love potion for my son . . . she makes him smile,’ he added.

‘It’s good to smile,’ replied the old woman.

‘The potion,’ said the king.

‘A snippet of snout of snake, I think, and a filet of fairly hairy fish, is it? No, that’s not quite right. Anti-love, that’s a squeezer. I doubt there’s a potion for such a thing. Perhaps if I take a bit of bat’s breath, or is it toe of mole? No, knee of newt, I think. . . .’

And while the king waited, the old woman squinted her eyes and scraped her jars and stirred her cauldron and eventually poured a portion of potion into a glass flask and handed it to the king.

‘You’re quite sure this will do the trick?’ asked the king.

‘No,’ said the old woman, ‘but it might. I’ve lost the tops to all my flasks,’ she continued. ‘Just hold it gently, and try not to spill it.’

‘What if it spills?’ asked the king.

‘Off you go now,’ she replied, and shooed him out the door.”

"The king rode back to the castle holding the flask in front of him. The horse occasionally shied at stirrings in the woods. Each time the horse shied, the king lost a portion of potion. And each time a drop spilled, events took place.

A small stone sprouted feet and began stomping crabgrass.

A raspberry grew as large as a watermelon, popped like a red balloon, and vanished.

A newt sunning himself by the trail turned into a tiny tenor and ran off to sing opera."

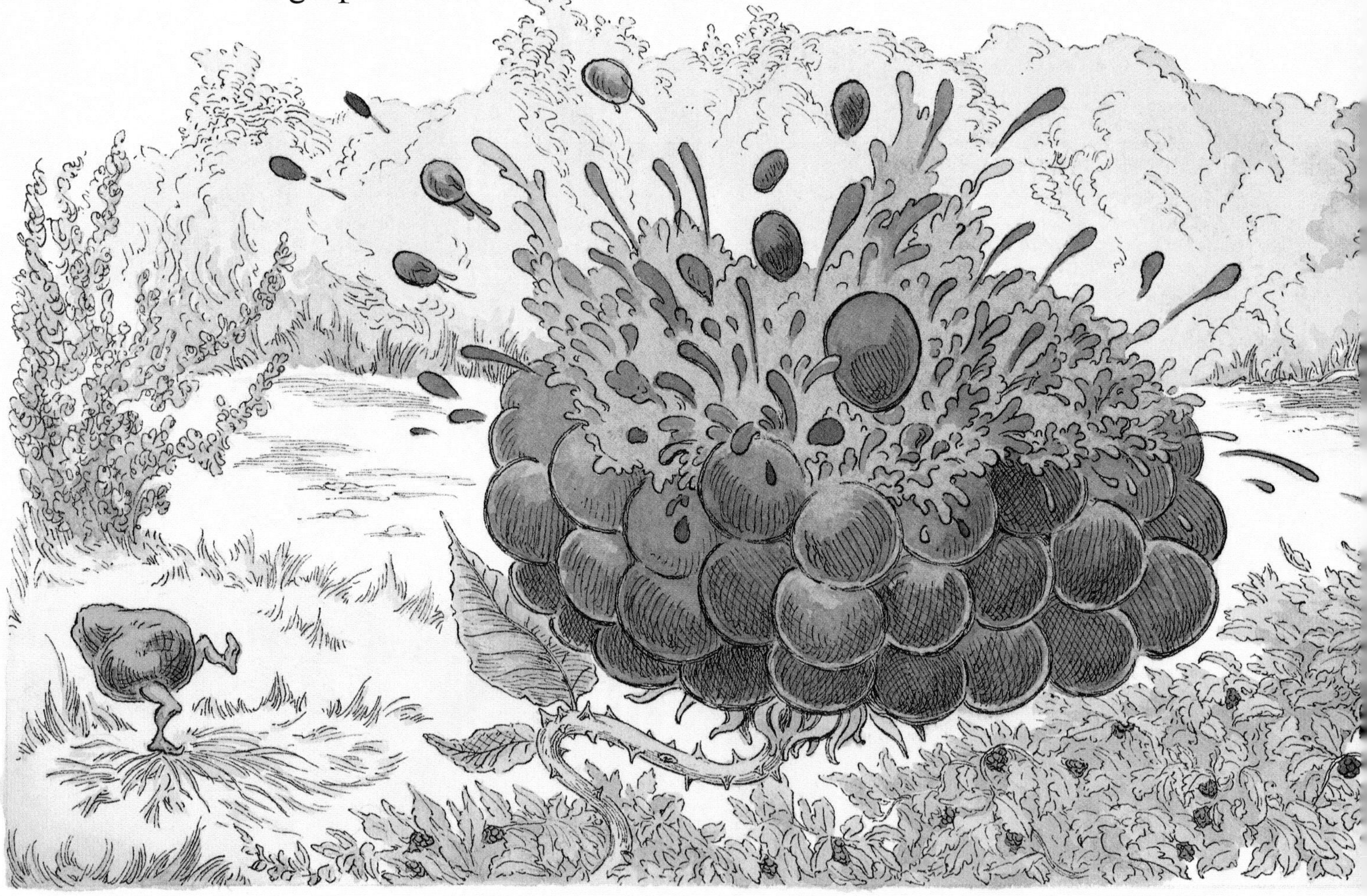

"As the king rode into the courtyard, the moon rose over the castle. Jaylee met the king and led his horse to water. The king thanked her, but he did not look into her eyes. He headed for his royal chambers and went straight to bed."

"The next morning the king poured the potion into his son's orange juice and crept back to bed. In the middle of breakfast, His Royal Highness the Prince turned into a frog and hopped away.

When the prince didn't show up to help feed the horses, Jaylee came around to the breakfast room. She peeked in the window and saw half a muffin and a sip of orange juice. But no prince. Jaylee finished off the juice. She slipped the muffin into the left front pocket of her frock and set off to find the prince."

"Halfway down the castle lane Jaylee lost her imagination. She blinked and looked around. The old woman's spell had worked, in a roundabout sort of way. Without imagination, Jaylee would never think of looking for her prince as a frog. Indeed, she would never think of looking for a prince. 'Oh dear,' she said, 'I must be late for school.'"

"Wait a minute," interrupted Jane. "Where's the part about the pond and the golden ball and I thought it was a princess who lived in a castle with her father and—"

"I thought you didn't read this kind of story," said the frog.

"Well, I'm starting to remember hearing about it. And if you think I'm going to kiss an amphibian, a slimy green frog, and forget about my muffin money—"

"Do you want to hear the end of the story or not?" interrupted the frog.

"I'm listening," said Jane. "It better be good."

"The end of the story is at the end of this stream," said the frog, and at that he leapt down the side of the stream. He leapt with high joyous leaps. Large leggy leaps. He leapt and leapt. Jane jumped up and ran after him on the opposite bank.

"I can't go very far," she called. "This better not be a trick!"

“Let’s pop the tops off dandelions and watch them float,” called the frog.

“Why?” Jane called back.

“Look at the sun on these leaves,” sang the frog. He stopped leaping to stare up at a jewelweed plant. Jane jumped across the stream and joined him. She bent down and looked. The leaves and stems glowed with the sun on them. She smiled.

Soon the ground became smoother, the stream gentler, and Jane's footsteps lighter. The frog made up a song, and Jane joined in on the chorus. She laughed at the last verse. They ran and leapt together now.

They had just invented a game of tag when, at a turn in the path, the frog leapt over a log and vanished down a hole. Jane peered into the hole. It was completely dark. She got on her hands and knees, and called down the hole. Her voice disappeared. She put an ear to the hole. It sounded black. An odd feeling crept its way up through her toes.

Jane *missed* the frog.

At that precise moment the ground shook. Horse chestnuts flew from the hole. Silver shot out, turned into half a muffin, and landed in the left front pocket of her frock. Jane vanished—and there stood Jaylee.

Jaylee blinked. The spell was broken. In front of Jaylee stood the prince. He smiled.

"I thought the princess had to *kiss* the frog," said Jaylee.

"You're not a princess. You had to *miss* me."

"Magnificent," said Jaylee. "I'd rather kiss you now, when you're not so green."

So she did . . . and happily ever after.